Moonlight & Mistletoe

JOHN MARINELLI

Table of Contents

Preface

Moonlight and Mistletoe is about two married couples, one couple that lived in the 18th century and another in the 21st century. Although they lived at different times in history, they both lived in the same town and in the same farmhouse.

They were from different worlds, with different lifestyles and different values. The modern couple somehow found themselves wishing they could be more like the couple from the past.

Both couples are joined together by a family journal, an actual record of a particular time in the lives of the couple from the past.

The aim of this book is to call attention to the power of God to direct one's destiny into a majestic flow of God's grace.

The storyline is the blending process that transforms two hearts and reshapes their desires.

Introduction

OUR STORY BEGINS WITH MOONLIGHT shining through the trees onto the porch of a little farmhouse in central Indiana. The year is 2020. Jim and Mary Travis are sitting on the porch swing and reading a family journal that dates back to the 1800s.

The journal is a record of the 50th wedding party of Mike and Laura Travis, Jim's great, great, grandparents. Mary is reading as Jim listens to the story unfold.

William, Mike and Laura's only child, wrote the journal after their passing 1935. It was a keepsake to be passed down from generation to generation. It's now in the hands of Jim Travis, the only living grandson.

The journal record covers a time period from the Civil War through the 1920s. It was written as a tribute to their lives and as a testimony to their Christian values.

The story in the journal begins when Mike and Laura were in their seventies. The year is 1920. They are looking back over the years and remembering how they met. It was a very romantic time and full of laughter over the silly things they both did while courting and being together.

Mary Reads The Journal's Introduction

My name is William P. Travis. I am writing this journal in the year 1937. I will be narrating this story. My knowledge is extensive as I am the only child of Mike and Laura Travis.

My parents could not have thought, not even in a million years, how they would ever stay together so long. They would always say, "If it hadn't been for the grace of God." Then they would laugh and hold one another close, giving thanks to God for helping them through the last 50 years.

My father would jokingly blame all the things that went wrong on the moonlight. He swore that the light from the full moon made him act so silly.

My mother, on the other hand, blamed the mistletoe that hung in the doorway every Christmas. She said it had a special romantic power that pulled her to my dad and kept her frazzled.

Chapter One

Moonlight Madness

J IM INTERRUPTING MARY, "I HAVE a question. What is it about moonlight that causes folks to believe in superstitions?"

Mary answers saying, "I was doing some research for a college paper last week and came across a book that talked about moonlight.

According to the 1944 Farmer's Almanac a person can have good luck during a full moon but not always. Bad luck is also a possibility. Here's what the Almanac says:

A Full Moon
Means Good Luck

- It is lucky to expose your newborn to the waxing Moon. It will give the baby strength.

- And it's also lucky to move into a new house

during the new Moon; prosperity will increase as the Moon waxes.

- It is lucky to see the first sliver of a new Moon "clear of the brush," or unencumbered by foliage.

- Ever wonder why people keep rabbit feet? It is lucky … especially if the rabbit was killed in a cemetery by a cross-eyed person at the dark of the Moon.

- It is lucky to hold a moonstone in your mouth at the full Moon; it will reveal the future.

- It is lucky to have a full Moon on the "Moon day" (Monday).

The Moon Can Also Bring Bad Luck,

- It is unlucky to have a full Moon on Sunday.

- It is unlucky to see the first sliver of a new Moon through a window; you'll break a dish.

- And it's certainly unlucky to sleep in the moonlight, or worse, be born in the moonlight!

- It is unlucky to point at the new Moon or view any Moon over your shoulder.

- It is unlucky to see "the old Moon in the arms of the new" or the faint image of the full disk while the new crescent Moon is illuminated, especially if you're a sailor. Storms are predicted.

Folklore has it that childbirth and even marriage are influenced by the Moon.

As the Moon regulates water, it's an age-old belief that it also regulates the rise and fall of our emotional tides.

According to some lore, the full Moon is an ideal time to accept a proposal of marriage as love is amplified. This certainly does not mean that marriages that do not happen on Full Moon nights are not successful – although it could be less than auspicious to get married when there's no Moon in the sky at all.

Further, the Full Moon is the best time to consummate marriage, according to the ancient Greeks, while the New Moon is the best time to drain out stale energy and belief systems.

The New Moon phase is also the one best for breaking up.

According to folklore, if a young woman sees a dove and glimpses the new Moon at the same instant, she should say: "Bright Moon, clear Moon, Bright and fair, Lift up your right foot, There'll be a hair." When she removes her

shoe, she'll find a hair the color of her future husband's."
(Source: 1944 Farmer's Almaniac)

Molonlight And Crazy

Mary continues her answer to Jim's question about moonlight madness. "Surely you have heard of a "Lunatic." You know, the crazy guy that is not all there. Luna means moon, a lunatic is one who has lost touch with reality and it is the moon's fault. Some would say that a lunatic is a moon-sick puppy.

However, being in the moonlight with your spouse or special someone is not crazy. Mike and Laura must have known this first hand.

According to the journal, they made it a habit to take a stroll two or three times a week in the light of the moon. It brought them closer together emotionally and kept their arguments down to a minimum. Moonlight madness was just what the doctor ordered.

"Let's get back to reading the journal."

Laura laughed when Mike blamed the moon for his shortcomings. She said, "You mean to tell me that your wild lifestyle and childish actions were a result of too much moonlight?"

Mike shrugged his shoulders and smiled saying, "Well yea! I was under a spell. I was moonstruck. Ever since the first time we held hands, I fell into a lovesick stuper. You were so gorgeous that I could not control my actions."

Laura laughted again and said, "You're Crazy" Mike replied, "See, it's the moonlight"

Laura couldn't leave it with Mike getting the last word so she began to formulate a "way back then" list of Mike's values. She wanted Mike to see himself then and now. He had changed a lot yet was still that crazy lovable guy.

She began with: "You used to say that there was no God. That wasn't the moonlight. It was your own belief that faded away over the years."

Mike agreed saying, "You are right. I started to believe in God when I saw His love flowing out of your spirit to me. I couldn't deny it. It was patient, kind, loving and full of forgiveness. It made me love you all the more and helped me to be a better person. I never knew God's love until you came into my life."

Laura was taken back by what Mike said. She was overjoyed and yet had no reply. There was complete silence for about a minute as Laura and Mike just looked at each other. Then Laura spoke saying, "It wasn't all God's love, you know? I was there too, loving you with all my heart. See, it took two of us to bring you to the truth."

So Laura and Mike went down memory lane together talking about the good life they shared with each other over the years. The moon rose up in the evening sky and disappeared behind a cloud. A cool breeze began to blow causing a chill in the air. It was time to call it a night and retire to the living room to sit by the fire.

Mike's Confession

Mike extended his hand to Laura and led her to the living room but did not sit down. He said, "There are some things I need to say before we get too far from memory lane."

Laura lovingly smiled and said, "OK"

Mike wanted Laura to know his heart, how he really felt inside. There had been many arguments over trivial things and sometimes even hard words were exchanged. Mike found it difficult expressing his inner most feelings but this night he knew he had to try.

He cleared his throat and began to speak saying, "I know that I was far from being a good husband when we were first married. My thinking was all messed up. I was a very liberal stinker. I was against most everything that was traditional and moral. How you ever put up with me, I'll never know."

"We argued a lot back then. I always admired you for standing up for what you believed. You were passionate about your values and pushed back when I threatened them with my immoral suggestions, like the time I wanted us to live together without being married or the time I wanted to steal a cow from our neighbor."

Laura's Godly Stand

"You told me, in no uncertain terms, that it was your way or the highway…that you were not going against God to be with me. He always came first.

You made me think about what I was saying and doing. I was forced to choose between you and my beliefs. The thing is, my core beliefs were based upon other folks expectations.

"I am so glad that I chose you and realized that God was not so bad after all. He's the good guy and worthy of my faith and trust. I turned my life around because I wanted what I saw in you. I saw Jesus and it changed me from the inside out.

Every time I hold your hand or kiss your lips or become close in any way, I feel joy and peace and love. It's a wonderful thing and it's because you stood up and didn't let my foolish heart rule over you.

I love everything about you and am pleased to have spent these almost 50-years together."

Laura was speechless. She heard words come from Mike that had never been spoken until that night. She could see his love for her beaming all around the room. It was like a bright glow emanating from his personality. Tears came to her eyes and she hugged him and they kissed.

Then Laura said, "See, it wasn't moonlight madness that

kept you in the darkness. It was the work of evil spirits that wanted your eternal soul to be damned with them in the day of God's judgment.

"The moonlight doesn't make you crazy. It instead makes you happy that you are alive and loved. That's why we spend so much time in the light of a silvery moon or in the glow of the harvest moon. It truly is a place for lovers to enjoy each other and to be romantic."

Mike agreed with Laura and they settled on the sofa continuing to talk. After all the deep emotional moments Mike changed the subject saying, "I hope William can get time off to be with us at our 50th anniversary party. He, and the grandkids will be shocked when we tell them we are planning to sell the farm and move away to a warmer climate.

Moving will require a lot of sacrifice and some major adjusting but it will allow us to enjoy our twilight years. You're still a good-looking woman and when I loose weight, I'll be gorgeous too.

Just think about it? Moving will put us in touch with lots of other retirees that have also moved from their homes all around the country. We will rub shoulders with New Yorkers, Canadians, Midwesterners, and even New Englanders.

That's going to be strange. Lots of different accents and ways of life mixed together in a retirement community way down south. I don't know if I will like that, now that I think about it. What do you think, Laura?"

Laura took a few moments to think about what Mike said and then replied, "I think it will be great. We will get to see how the rest of the country lived over the same years that we spent on this farm. It will be a fun time to share stories and romantic interludes."

Mike agreed and they moved on to other topics. He looks at the fireplace and said, "How about if I make a fire and you do the hot tea thing? Then we can cuddle by the fire-light with a blanket. It's getting colder out.

The season is changing again. I can't keep up with them anymore. I just get settled in summer and it turns into fall, then winter and spring and back to summer again. I am going to enjoy not having seasons to worry about. I hear it is always sunny and warm down south."

Laura laughed and said, "I hear that it gets cold there too just not as severe. All in all, we'll have a great time meeting new folks, sharing old stories from our past and drinking iced tea."

Mike started to think more about moving and was over-whelmed. He looks at Laura and says, "What do we do with all this stuff? We will have to have a huge sale and we'll have to sell our wagons and horses and livestock and what about the dogs?"

Laura feels Mike's panic and tries to calm him down saying, "Wait a moment. We don't have to do this today or even tomorrow. It is going to take a while for us to get it all together. Don't freak out on me now."

Mike calmed down and they resume their cuddling by the fireplace.

Chapter Two

The Mistletoe Waltz

IKE NEVER UNDERSTOOD WHY LAURA would not go with him to the Mistletoe Waltz. He had asked her every year and she always said no. They did go together once when they were engaged.

The waltz was a few months away and was the biggest dance in the area. It was full of big named people who were the movers and shakers of their community. He wanted to "hob knob" but Laura would not go. Mike felt left out because there was good food, a great band and even fireworks. Everyone who was anybody would be there and he wanted to be somebody important.

So Mike blurted it out again. "How about we go to the Mistletoe Waltz this year? Remember the last time we were there? It was a lot of fun."

Laura was annoyed by Mikes request. She replied, "I sure do. You made a fool of yourself in front of 250 people.

You had too much to drink and really got out of hand. You kept asking me to marry you and kept telling me that you were in love with me. I was so embarrassed."

Mike didn't remember the details of that night. It had been over 50 years since they danced together under the mistletoe. He was surprised that Laura remembered. He tried to make light of it saying, "Yeah but we were just kids. It was a long time ago. I finally felt grown up and wanted to have fun. Plus, I wasn't chasing after that other girl. She was chasing me. It must have been my new overalls and stripped shirt."

Now Mike knew why they never attended another Mistletoe Waltz. It was that girl who he didn't even know and all that free beer he consumed. So Mike softly said, "Is it too late to say I am sorry?"

Laura felt sorry for Mike and quickly responded by saying, "No it's not too late. I will forgive you and let it go but you have to do more than just say you are sorry."

Mike was relieved but also puzzled. He timidly said, "more! Like what?"

Laura started to laugh and told him, " No more beer for a week; cook supper for the next 3-days; or just love me always with your entire being."

Mike also laughed and said, "Deal to the love always thing and we'll go to town to a fancy restaurant. Cooking and me don't get along."

Now Laura was concerned because Mike's idea of a favorite restaurant was The Beer Barn where he could get a large chili and a loaf of cheese bread. That wasn't her idea of a special night out.

So, Laura said, "How about a trip to that new steakhouse just outside of town?

Mike agreed but with one condition. He said, "Ok but I get to drive. My leg is better now."

Mike, The Deer And The Rabbit

"I know what you're going to say. I shouldn't have messed with that deer in the nearby field. But it looked like it was real tame, I thought it would be ok until I got too close and it kicked me. It was a crazy thing to do."

Laura knew that Mike always did crazy things. She remembered the time when he chased the baby rabbit. He ran all over the yard, knocking down two flowerpots, one lawn chair and a ladder. It was silly things like that that caused Laura to stay with Mike so long. He always made her laugh. She thought to herself, "he is just too cute to be mad at." Then she said it out loud. "You are just too cute to be mad at."

Mike loved Laura more than anything. He was glad that she was not really angry with him. He told her, "It's my job to make you laugh and see that you are happy. That's why I was created, just for you. I'll bet that God made me so He could laugh too."

Laura smiled and said, "Don't get too puffed up. Now and then is good but I don't want you to get carried away trying to perform for God."

I've Got A Secret

Laura had a secret that she was dying to tell Mike. She had kept it to herself for three months but it was now just too heavy to hold. She told Mike that she wanted to get back to planning their 50th wedding party. She called out to Mike and walked over to the sofa and said, "We are going to have a very special guest at our wedding party, I think."

Now the secret was out. Mike said, "Who's coming to dinner that is so special?" Mike's curiosity was peaked and he said "Anybody I know?"

Laura was glad that she could finally tell Mike and so she did. "Well I am not absolutely sure but my girlfriend at church knows a friend of one of the assistants to the Governor. She said that his relatives live just down the road from our church. She's going to ask her friend to ask the assistant to ask the Governor to drop by and wish us a happy wedding anniversary. That could happen, you know. It's not too far out, is it?"

Mike laughed to himself and told her, "Yes babe, it could

happen but not before hell freezes over. The Governor has no interest in us. We're just little folks from the farm and he is, well, certainly not little."

The possible visit by the Governor was now out in the open and started to spread like wildfire among Mike and Laura's friends. They were all hoping to get an invitation so they could meet the big politician. The problem was, there was no reality in the rumor. Everyone heard the same story and knew that it was far fetched and yet they still believed it.

Arguments And The Sun

Mike and Laura were lovers of life and the pursuit of happiness. They argued a lot and made up a lot. They had a rule that said they could not let the sun go down upon their wrath.

It was a Bible expression that came from Ephesians 4:26 ***"Be ye angry, and sin not: let not the sun go down upon your wrath"***

So they would stay up all night if necessary until their problems were resolved. If the sun went down the lights went on. It would be ok quickly or last all night but it would always get worked out with a hug and a kiss.

Mistletoe And Romance

Now Laura loved the smell of Mistletoe and made sure

she had some every year during the holidays. She felt that it was romantic and had power to generate unsolicited romantic advances. She swore that it was the mistletoe that drew her to Mike in the beginning.

She didn't see it as a spell but rather a gentle nudge towards expressing what was already inside. That notion proved to be true as Mike saw the mistletoe and called Laura's attention to it as he asked her for a kiss.

He said, "It's the law, you know. If a couple stands under the mistletoe, they are bound by love to kiss and if they kiss, it will ignite a flame in their souls that no other can extinguish."

So Mike called upon Laura, way back when they first met, to plant a kiss on his lips and she did and the flame still burns brightly after all these years.

Today they both laugh saying, "If it wasn't for the mistletoe" Mike and Laura have a lot of "If it wasn't for the" statements.

1. If it wasn't for the mistletoe.

2. If it wasn't for Ephesians 4:26.

3. If it wasn't for the grace of God.

4. If it wasn't for the moonlight.

Laura tossed another log on the fire and cuddled again

with Mike. They loved being together. The firelight and the crackling of burning wood made their time together perfect. They were both lovers and best friends.

The Dream From Hell

That night Laura had a dream in which she saw herself and Mike dancing at the Mistletoe Waltz. As she looked around the dance floor she noticed that all the couples were her classmates from high school. It was a scary feeling as most of them had passed away years ago. Some dies in the War, some in various accidents and some from illnesses.

As they danced she recognized the tune of the song that the band played. It was "The Pine Tree Waltz."

Laura woke up in a cold sweat. She began to cry because she saw her lover falling to his death and she wanted the waltz and their marriage to last forever. She thought it was a preminition that was about to actually happen. She began to tremble until Mike woke up and began to comfort her. She held him close and said, "I don't want you to die. We have to go to the to Mistletoe Waltz and dance together."

Mike was confused and asked her why, considering she refused all the other years. Then Laura shared her dream with him.

Mike began to laugh and said, "You're not getting rid of me that easy. I am in perfect health except for all those things that are going wrong. They are minor. No big stuff yet and it will be years before I die."

Now Laura was a woman of faith. She began to explain, "I need to go and dance so I can prove that dream to be false. It is a lie from the pit of hell and I will not entertain it. By dancing at the Mistletoe Waltz, we will prove the dream to be wrong."

So Mike agreed and they made plans to get tickets as soon as they came up for sale. Mike fell back to sleep and Laura got up, trying to shake off the terrible vision she had just seen.

She put on the tea kettle and settled into her favorite chair with her Bible. As she opened it, her eyes fell upon a particular scripture. It said,

"You will live a long life. With long life I will satisfy him, And show him My salvation." (Psalm 91:16)

Laura felt that God was speaking directly to her about her relationship with Mike and their life together. She thanked the Lord for His word and went back to sleep in Mike's arms.

Tomorrow was a new day and Laura knew that God's mercies were new every morning. She was again at peace and thankful to God for His comfort.

Chapter Three

Lovers On Parade

IKE AND LAURA WERE LIKE "Lovers On Parade." They were so in love with each other that it showed like a billboard to everyone around them.

One night at a social gathering they were dancing as they usually do and a group of ladies commented to them, saying, "You must be newly weds" They just laughed and told the ladies that they had been married for many years.

Oozing Love

It was that special love inside Mike and Laura that kept oozing out when they least expected it. Folks couldn't help but take notice. Laura knew that it was the Love of God that shined brightly in her soul.

Some ladies were actually jealous and didn't like Laura because she was so happy. Their husbands were not like hers. Mike was no saint but he was in many ways. He put

Laura first is everything. He lived for her, whereas, the other husbands around him lived for themselves.

Laura did the same. She put Mike first before herself. This was the real secret of their long life and happy marriage. They did not live for themselves but each other.

Doing The Right Thing

Mike and Laura practiced doing what God instructed them to do in the Bible.

Things like *"Be kindly affectionate one to another with brotherly love; in honor preferring one another."* Romans 12:10

Now Laura knew that Romans 12:10 was referring to the treatment of brothers in Christ but she also saw it as a pathway for her. Mike was a brother in Christ and qualified for her brotherly love in addition to her romantic love.

So Laura and Mike lived for each other's scarification. If they didn't agree as touching a certain thing, big or small, they dropped it like a hot potato. There was no "Rule Over Me" mentality.

Mike was always the head of the family and responsible to God for its well-being. However, that didn't make Laura a slave. She was created by God as the other side of man and played a vital role in helping him to fulfill the destiny of God for the family. Laura would often say, God created man as male and female, not just male. She saw herself as an equal part of that creation.

$\mathcal{B}ible \ \mathcal{B}ased \ \mathcal{G}uidance$

Mike and Laura loved the Bible and especially the King James Version. Yes, it was sometimes hard to understand because of the old English but still poetic and more powerful in its presentation. They still referred to more modern translations but always held the KJV as their primary source.

Both Mike and Laura would hide key scriptures in their hearts so they could call upon them at a moment's notice. If a situation came up that needed the application of wisdom or special handling, they would search their hearts first to recall God's word. Then they would go to the scriptures if they didn't have the answer.

This memorization kept them from inadvertently falling into an evil trap. Mike used this methodology most often to avoid sexual fantasies that led him into a lustful heart. If his eyes fell upon another woman to lust, he would turn away and look for a scripture to hang on to.

His most used scripture was one of the Ten Commandments,

"You shall not covet your neighbor's wife, or his male or female servant, his ox or donkey, or anything that belongs to your neighbor." Deuteronomy 5:21

Unlike the other commandments, which focused on outward actions, this commandment focused on thought. It is an imperative against setting one's desire on things that are forbidden.

Mike felt if he could at least try to follow what God wanted, he would be better off as a person and as a husband. So he decided from the beginning of his marriage that he would not be the kind of a man that looked and desired other women. He made Laura the object of his affection and coveted her.

It's hard for a man to be oblivious to female flirting, advances and sexual innuendos. However, Mike was most of the time because his focus was on his own woman. He didn't have time to fanaticize about what life would be like with some other female. If he did get caught up in a fantasy, he would ask himself one simple question, "What does she have that Laura does not provide?" The answer was always, nothing.

Laura was head and shoulders above other women because she was committed to her husband and made it known to him and everyone else nearly every day.

Laura's Concerns

As time passed on from Laura's terrible dream, Mike and she got back on track for planning their wedding renewal party. Laura pulled Mike away from his farm duties with a cup of coffee and a fresh apple pie. They sat down on the porch as before waiting for the moon to rise in the sky and its light to shine their way.

Laura said to Mike, "We have a lot of decisions to make and not much time to make them. Here are my concerns:

1. "Are we really going to sell our farm?   It's been in the family since the 1700s.

2. Do we really want to move to Florida? There will be no family there. We will be all alone in a new place.

3. What about William and grandbabies? They will miss being around us.

4. Do you still want to spend all that money for a wedding party when we are moving? Maybe we shouldn't."

Mike listened carefully to what Laura was saying and lovingly replied. "I want whatever makes us happy. If it's moving, that will be great. If it's staying, that's ok too. Whatever we do, it must be a blessing from God. We do not want to step out of His will. I know that He will let us know where to go, if at all, when the time comes. Until then, we just keep on keeping on being happy."

Laura agreed and said, "The matter at hand is a wedding party and that is just about finalized."

Jim and Mary took a break from reading to discuss all that Mike and Laura had said in the journal. Mary was amazed, saying, "These things happened over 100 years ago. It's like we went back in time to their day and watched them live."

Jim said, "It's like watching a movie in my mind. I feel like I am there as one of their friends. It's weird too because they are my great, great, grandparents."

Mary responded, "Maybe our life together will be put in a journal and passed down through the family."

Jim said," What's so special about us? We're just a struggling young couple trying to get through college and find a good job. We're just ordinary people. My great, great, grandparents were pioneers."

Mary interrupted Jim by saying, "No they weren't. The pioneers were in the 17th century. You ancestors were ordinary people just like us trying to earn a living in a world of economic hardships. They were farmers like the whole Travis clan."

Mary opens the journal and says, "let's read some more."

The Whisper In The Wind

"Listen, do you hear it?" said Laura. "Hear what?" said Mike.

Laura said, "Be quiet and listen. I can hear the rolling thunder and the flapping of eagle's wings way off in a distance." "I don't hear anything." said Mike. "Anyway, what does that mean?"

"Only this", said Laura. " It's going to be a cold winter and WAR is on the horizon. We will have to be like the eagle, keeping a sharp eye out for trouble and always ready to soar above the difficulties that come our way. I see it in the Spirit and feel it in my soul. It's like that poem the pastor read in church."

With Eagles' Wings

I mounted up with Eagles' Wings
to soar above the clouds.
I viewed life above its trials,
separate from the crowds.

Just me and God, together in the day,
His love to behold.
With Eagles' Wings, He led the way,
my future to unfold.

Forgiveness and peace in a distance,
suddenly I could see.
Joy and happiness trailed behind
then overshadowed me.

With Eagles' Wings,
I soar above life's every trial.
Now I walk by word of faith,
rejoicing with every mile.

By: John Marinelli

"So what's whispering in the wind?" said Mike.

"It's the Spirit of God telling us to soar above the stress of this life and fly with Him", said Laura.

"Don't you see, our Lord wants us to draw nigh to Him. That means get closer. Don't stray away because of other folk's expectations or criticisms.

We need to focus on the things of God and His promises. We need to share our faith with others and tell them that God loves them just as much as He loves us.

God will whisper in the wind. If we are not listening for His voice, we will miss His guidance."

"So what does all of this have to do with our 50th wedding party?" said Mike.

"Only this" said Laura. "We will have all our friends and all our neighbors at our party. We do not want to be re-membered for a big beer bash and leave a shameful stain on our Christian testimony.

We must invite Jesus to our party and let it be known that we hold His truth dear to our hearts.

It doesn't have to be a church service. But it does have to be respectful of our Lord. That means, No alcohol, No cigars and No moonshine. We will dance, laugh and enjoy all the fixins. It's our party and if anyone doesn't like it, they can stay home."

Mike replies by saying, "You are right. If we can't live as

Christians, there is no need to pretend. This will show us who our real friends are and what values they hold dear."

Mary stops reading to make a comment. "Boy, your great, great, grandparents were tough. They were willing to loose all, some or most of their friends over alcohol. It wouldn't even be an issue in today's world. Nobody cares what you do. It's like, do your own thing and let me do mine."

Jim also comments. "I think it's great that they had a value system and were willing to stand for what they believed. If we did the same, we'd be called religious fanatics.

My great, great, grandparents didn't care what other people thought. They lived their own lives and blazed their own trail in accordance with what God showed them. Now that's great."

Chapter Four

Wine, Women And Uh-Oh

S O MARY GOES BACK TO reading the journal and Jim sits back to take it all in. Hearing Mary read about a family member from 100 years ago was amazing. He just couldn't get enough. He wanted to know how it all ended but not before he learned more about their lives.

Now Mike, before Laura, was a lady's man. He was tall, over 6-feet, dark hair with a streak of white in the front. It was a distinguishing mark that set him aside to be noticed for sure. He had that streak from age sixteen and all the gals liked it.

Mike may have been a farm boy but he sure could dance. He did a mean 2-step and could waltz with the best of' them.

The, "Uh-Oh Man"

As Mike became a young man, he began to make his own

wine. He also danced with lots of girls and gained a repu-tation of the "Uh-oh" man.

Good girls knew to be on guard when Mike passed their way and when they saw him with a new girl, they auto-matically said, "UH-OH", we need to talk to her.

Laura was one of the girls that said, "Uh Oh" but thought that Mike was really good looking. One Christmas, she found herself standing under the mistletoe on a moonlit night. She was waiting for one of her girlfriends when Mike strolled up and said, "Kiss Me." She said, "I will not. Who do you think you are, anyway?"

The Rule of The Mistletoe

Mike replied, "My name is Mike Travis and you are now with me under the mistletoe on a moonlit night. The rule is, if you are asked to kiss a fella, you must comply be-cause, well, it's the rule of the mistletoe."

So Laura said, "Well I guess I have to comply. I don't want to break the rule of the mistletoe." Then she kissed Mike and both were immediately swept off their feet into a strange moonlight madness, otherwise known as falling in love.

All the other, "Uh-Oh" girls that saw Mike and Laura kissing began to gossip and tell stories that were not true. They were jealous and mad at themselves for not standing under the mistletoe.

So Laura shacked up with Mike, helped him make lots of wine and they both became town drunks.

"Wait a minute, Mary. That's not what happened or did it, for real?" said Jim.

Mary laughed and said, "I just wanted to see if you were paying attention. No that's not what happened. Instead, they really did fall in love and were married that same year, August of 1870."

According to the journal, the "Uh-oh" girls went on criticizing Laura and pining over Mike. Laura walked away with the "Uh-oh" man and that was that.

Two Little Wine Makers

Laura did, however, help Mike make wine. They grew grapes and made wine and homemade jellies. Their little farm grew into the Buck Creek Winery and for over 40 years their wine was the best that Indiana had to offer.

Laura commented to Mike, saying, "I feel bad that my girlfriends are telling stories about me and talking behind my back. I didn't do anything to them. I just fell in love with you. That's not a crime, is it?"

Mike says, "Not in my book. I dated most of those girls and they weren't nearly as nice as you. I am sure that their critical attitudes are because you captured my heart and they didn't. It also could be because we make wine and still profess to be Christians."

Laura replied, "Didn't the apostle Paul tell Timothy to take a little wine for his stomach?

Here it is in I Timothy 5:12 *Drink no longer water, but use a little wine for thy stomach's sake and thine often infirmities.*

See, it's not evil to drink a little wine. What is evil is to become a winebibber. That's a drunk.

God blessed us with a farm and a vineyard. If the, "Uh-Oh" girls don't like it, it's just too bad. We answer to God, not them."

Mike replied, "Well, no matter now anyway. We sold the vineyard over 10 years ago. It served its purpose. We used most of the income to support foreign missionaries and help our local church to meet its financial needs and that's a good thing."

Laura made another wine comment. "Remember the wine tasting party we put on for the church during foreign missions week? You set up several pots full of wine in the fellowship hall and after dinner we all got to taste the wine."

"That's right", said Mike. " I started with a lower grade wine and used an average grade and then used the best wine we made.

We demonstrated the water into wine miracle that Jesus did at the wedding feast. All the guests thought that the best was held for last. Only the disciples knew it was just made fresh by Jesus."

Mary stops reading to say, "Yeah, and the wine in your great, great, grandparent's day, like in Biblical times was not processed to increase the alcohol level. Today's wine is far more potent than back then."

Jim agreed and Mary went back to reading.

Women On Parade

Mike looked over at Laura and said, "Of all the women I have known, you are the very best."

Laura replied to Mike's comment by saying, "And how many women did you know back then? Let's see, there was Martha, Judy, Sue, Mary Jo, Catherine, Annie, and oh yeah, Lois. Did I miss anyone?"

Mike said, "A few but no matter. It was long ago. Those days were fun but I did the wild oats thing and settled down with you. The women were just a, "Pass The Time Away Thing", until I came across that special gal of my dreams.

It's like Adam and God in the Garden of Eden. God brought the animals to Adam for naming. He did so and in the process noticed that they were male and female. He also noticed that there was no female for him. I think he was looking through all the animals for his female but did not find her.

Then God caused a deep sleep to fall upon Adam. Then He brought forth Eve and presented her to Adam. First thing out of his mouth was, "Well now, this is flesh of my flesh and bone of my bones."

He saw that he didn't have to settle for animals to meet his needs. God gave him His very best, a woman.

"So it was with me. I was tired of looking through all the animals for a mate. But God brought you to me and I saw, for the first time, *"Bone of My Bones And Flesh of My Flesh.* Now that's my story and I am sticking to it."

Laura laughed and said, "So I am your flesh and bone. Well, guess what? There is more to me than that. I have a soul and a mind and a will of my own. I am the other side of you. I am you in a skirt. But I know what you are trying to say, I think.

You found yourself in me and saw in me qualities that would complete you and make you the man that God wanted you to be. So, without woman, man cannot be man because man was created male and female. Laura laughs and said, it's great to feel needed."

"Then the LORD God made a woman from the rib he had taken out of the man, and he brought her to the man. The man said, "This is now bone of my bones and flesh of my flesh; she shall be called 'woman,' for she was taken out of man." Genesis 2:23-24

Mike also laughed and said, "I don't know where I end and you begin. We are so intertwined that we almost think as one. It's weird isn't it? Sometimes I say what you are thinking before you speak it out and you do that to me as well. That must be the fulfillment of Genesis 2:24?"

"Therefore shall a man leave his father and his mother, and shall cleave unto his wife: and they shall be one flesh."

Laura replies, "You better believe it. That's why I have cleavage, so you can cleave."

Mary pauses her reading and smiled at Jim saying, "So, you want to cleave?" Jim laughed and said, "What, in front of my great, great, grandparents? At least close the journal."

Then they laughed, hugged and enjoyed the rest of the afternoon together.

A Shocking Revelation

The next morning Jim and Mary resumed their reading of the journal. Mary began with a shocking event that happened to Mike during his Civil War days.

Mike was a Captain in the Confederate Army. He had ties to the South even though Indiana was a strong supporter of the Union. He was also a Union spy that kept the North up to date with Yankee troop movements and helping captured Union soldiers to escape. He could have been shot as a trader if caught.

Mike worked with a Mary Edwards Walker, known for her unconventional dress - she often wore trousers and a man's coat - this pioneer physician worked for the Union army as a nurse and spy while she waited for an official commission as a surgeon.

Mike and Mary were more than friends and had a secret love affair during their service as Union spies. However, the secret love affair was not the shocking revelation. It was not so shocking because it was before Mike met Laura.

What was shocking was that Jim's Mary in the 21st century, who was reading the journal, was a direct decendant of Mary Edwards Walker who lived during the Civil War days.

Mary was named after her great, great, aunt who did serve as a scrgon in the Civil War. She started as a nurse and finally obtained her commision as a surgeon.

Jim said, "Let's review the facts. The question at hand is, are we related from a secret love affair that happened in the Cilil War or are we just a maried couple with a coincidence?"

Mary said, "Let me look for my family tree chart to see how far back it goes." She was, after all, Mary Elizabeth Walker before she was Mary E. Travis.

Mary finds the family tree chart and reads it to Jim. "I can't believe it. Mary Edwards Walker is my great, great, aunt. It says here that she served as a surgeon and saved many lives. After the Civil War, she married Mr. Willian J. Walker of North Carolina and they settled in Charlotte.

Mr. Walker was a land baron that owned several plantations in the Carolinas. He grew tobacco and owned a large textile factory.

Mary Travis was indeed a direct decendant of Mary Edwards Walker which meant that she and Jim had a connection that went beyond their wedding vows.

So Mary and Jim went back to the journal with a deeper interest in learning more about this Mike Travis of the 1800s. Mary begins again to read.

Mike said to Laura when she asked about his past, before she came into his life, "Let's keep the past in the past. It was war and I did things that were required of me by my country. Some assignments were not things that I am proud of. Nevertheless I had to do them."

Laura said ok to Mike's request but was that much more curious as to those things that happened. She said to herself, "Did he kill a lot of people? Did he dishonor his family or nation? Did he have several women before me?"

She would never know. The subject was closed, at least for now. So Laura decided to toss the ball of couriousity back into Mike's lap. She said, "I guess that applies to me as well. I don't have to come clean about my sorted past before I met you, right?"

Mike replied, "You don't have a sorted past. You were an, "Uh-Oh" girl, remember? But in any event, I can live with not knowing your, "Sorted" past."

Chapter Five

Blur By Design

MIKE HAS BLURRED THE PAST by design. He didn't want anyone to know that he was a, "Turncoat" posing as a confederate Captain but really a lieutenant in the Union army. Nor did he want anyone to know that he was deeply entwined in a secret love affair.

Mike was raised as a Baptist. That meant that he was schooled in the fundamentals of Bible truth and drilled in the, "How To" methods of Bible promise application. He knew right from wrong and had a very sensitive conscience.

The Trapped Soul

Not a day went by that Mike didn't feel bad about his secret love affair and his secret identity. His conscience bore witness to his immorality and deception.

One day, Mike looked into the mirror while dressing and

said to himself, "You are a liar, a cheat and a despicable individual. I hate you."

Mike struggled with guilt and shame and thought seriously about ending his life. His past wrong doings were getting the best of him.

The Remedy For Guilt And Shame

Then Mike's memory took him back to a place in time when he was a little boy sitting in church. He could see himself, with his mind's eye, rehearsing Bible passages. The adult teacher said that the children had to hide the Word of God in their hearts so they do not sin against God.

Suddenly it was very clear what the problem was and the source of the guilt. However, knowing why did not nulify the sin. It still lingered over his soul bringing condemnation.

Mike began to pray saying,

"Dear God, have mercy

on me, for I am a sinner.

Forgive me, oh my God

For having a wicked heart.

Cleanse me, dear Lord

From my Shame."

Suddenly Mike felt better, as though a heavy weight had lifted off of him. The guilt was gone. Mike knew that his prayer was answered and he had been forgiven. He was finally free from the past. Now he could look towards the future with a new perspective. Then he remembered a scripture passage that confirmed all that he felt. He began to recite it out loud.

"If we confess our sins, he is faithful and just to forgive us our sins, and to cleanse us from all unrighteousness." I John 1:9

Mike walked away that day a forgiven man, He had been cleansed and made whole. He began a new life that centered in God's will and doing good wherever he could.

Mary stopped reading. Tears fell from her face. Jim said, "What's wrong, honey?" She kept crying and began to sob. Jim, like most men, have no clue what's going on in the female mind. He kept asking Mary what was bothering her.

Finally Mary composed herself enough to explain. She said, " When I read what Mike went through, I thought it was me. I have suffered so long with guilt and shame. It overwhelms me at times and torments me every day. I need to talk to God"

Jim tried to cheer her up sayng, "Everything will be ok. Just go on with your life and forget the past. When you feel better, you can tell me what you did that was so bad"

Mary began to cry again and said, "Leave me alone." She closed the journal and went inside the farmhouse. Life had been a blur for her for many years, since high school and she hurt inside. She ran away from it but it followed her and tormented her every waking moment.

Mary was finally alone in her bedroom. She opened the journal to Mike's prayer and cried out to God. She read the prayer as if it were her own words. She became a sinner seeking forgiveness. Tears ran down her cheeks. Sobbing filled the room as Mary sought the Lord.

Suddenly, just like Mike's experience, Mary stopped crying and stood up and felt better. The weight of her past sin was gone and the suffering was gone. The torment stopped because she knew her prayers had also been answered. She was forgiven. She left her bedroom a new person.

Jim was waiting on the porch, afraid to enter the farmhouse until Mary said it was ok. Mary saw Jim and rushed to him and hugged him. He said, "Are you ok?" She replied, "Yes, I am ok. Better than ok. I have been forgiven."

Jim couldn't help but ask, "From what?" but Mary said, like Mike, I want to leave all that stuff in the past. I am ready to go on."

Like Laura, Jim was left to guess or wonder what all went on. He would never know unless Mary would share her secret sins from the past with him. Somehow he was ok with that. It wasn't that important now that his wife was free and more attentive to him.

Truth & Consequence

The next day, Mary and Jim came back to the swing on the porch with their iced tea and began to read again in the journal.

It's one thing to be forgiven by God and another to escape the consequences of sin. It's like getting in an argument that turns into a fight that ends in a broken nose. The guy that broke your nose can say he is sorry and you can forgive him but your nose is still broken. That is true of every action. There is a reaction that may occur. Sometimes the reaction can be hidden but most times not.

So it was with Mike. His actions caused a pregnancy that blossomed into a 100 year linage of ancestors that carried his DNA. They all have Travis blood flowing through their veins, including Mary of the 21st century. The mark of sin follows Mike's decendants through the years leaving a stain on their heritage.

However, what evil man may do sometimes get turned into a blessing by God. So it was with Mary and Jim. They found in each other a life of love and a quality of happiness that few couples ever see. They are truly following in the footsteps of Mike and Laura.

As Jim and Marry settled on the swing so did Mike and Laura. Both are planning out their future. One couple has already lived a lifetime while the other has just begun.

More than 100 years separate them but there seems to be a oura associated with the journal and the farmhouse swing that joins them together.

Mike and Laura begin again talking about their 50th wedding party while Jim and Mary discuss their apparent joint ancestry. As Mary reads the journal, Mike can hear Laura's voice saying,

"Now we have too many guests. The barn will hold only 100 people and we have request for 150. It's that darn rumor that the Governor is going to attend. What do we do now?"

Mike replies, "We'll still have it here and expand the party in and outside the barn. We'll rent tents and add them to the barn entrance."

Meanwhile the sun is going down and the moon is rising over the farmhouse in the 21st century. A chill is in the air and the light of the moon is inching up onto the porch where Jim and Mary are seated.

Jim stops Mary from reading to proclaim his newly found family connection. He says, "Mary! We are distant cousins or is it distant grandkids? My great, great, grandfather and your great great aunt came together to produce an offspring that produced a family that produced us. We have the same great, great, grandfather but different great, great, grandmothers."

Mary joins in by saying, "That makes us a really grand

couple, doesn't it? That knowledge and one dollar will get you a large soda at Mc Donalds."

So Jim and Mary settle on the porch swing in the moonlight as Mary continues reading the family journal. "Hey, look at this. There is a picture of Mary Edwards Walker."

Mary Edwards Walker

(November 26, 1832 – February 21, 1919), commonly referred to as Dr. Mary Walker, was an American abolitionist, prohibitionist, prisoner of war and surgeon. She is the only woman to ever receive the Medal of Honor.

"She was some lady and I am a direct descendant. How cool is that?"

Meanwhile back in the pages of the journal, Mary discovers another revelation about Mike Travis. She continues to read, personal entry: Mike Travis April 14th 1865.

"During my enlistment in the confederate army as a Captain, I played out the role of a military intelligence officer. In doing so, I discovered a plot to kidnap Abraham Lincoln by John Wilkes Booth.

I had to warn the President but could not get through the Union lines, even though I was a Union spy. They didn't believe me.

My confederate uniform was not convincing enough to the Union guards. They just captured me and marched me towards their prisoner stockade from which I promptly escaped.

I was helpless, said Mike, to save the President. Later I learned that the kidnapping turned into the assassination of President Abraham Lincoln at the Ford Theater.

The journal entry proved that Mike Travis was indeed a spy. Laura never read the journal so she never knew about Mike's past."

Mike and Laura leave the swing for a walk in the moonlight. He looks over at Laura and says, "Life is often a blur by design. It is for us anyway. We stumbled through the Civil War with all its intrigue, tragedy and even sickness and yet somehow we seemed to take it all in our stride.

The past was the past, good or bad. Now is now and worth living. Tomorrow may never come but we plan for it anyway and look forward with great hope that our times will be in our own hands and not at the mercy of another."

Laura responds, "I love you no matter what. We will make it through with God's help and we will see the blessings of our marriage in the lives of our children and their children."

As the moon shined down upon Mike and Laura they pledged themselves, once again, to each other and to the Lord. Laura said, "Our hope is in the Lord. He is our life-source and our assurance that the future will be a good one."

Laura Remembers And Laughs

"Let's sit by the lake and rest a while", said Mike. Laura agreed and they sat on a bench near the water." The moonlight shining off the water and the cool breeze drew them closer together to keep warm.

Laura starts to laugh and Mike asked her why she was laughing. She said, "Because I remembered our wedding day and how you were all dressed up in overalls and a bow tie with a straw hat. It was the funniest thing I had ever seen."

Mike responded by laughing too and saying, "Well, we didn't have money for a beautiful wedding dress and a shinny new suit. I had to use what I had. However, I though the corncob pipe made an excellent add on. It was funny even so."

Laura laughed at he idea of a corncob pipe. She said, "I was glad you didn't light it up. The guest thought you were hilarious. You made our wedding certainly unusual. We were the talk of the town for a month or so."

Mike said, "Yeah, I was famous. Everyone treated me like a big star. They even took pictures."

"I can't wait until my new overalls arrive. I ordered them from a catalog special for my upcoming wedding"

Laura responds to Mike's "One Minute" of fame. "Yeah, you were a star. You even got in the Pine Tree Gazette with a photo and short announcement. But that didn't make you a star.

"You are a star because you loved me. I am your biggest fan."

Chapter Six

Love Songs That Never Die

MIKE SAYS, "REMEMBER THE LOVE songs that we shared over the years.? How about this one, *Love's A Dream Of Mighty Treasure.* We danced a lot to that one."

"Here's another, Ah! How Sweet It Is To Love. It was our favorite. Remember Laura? Every time we kissed, for months, I'd say, How Sweet It Is. It was great. We'd kiss and laugh and kiss again. I loved those days."

Laura responds, "We need to start singing again and kissing after every song. What happened to our romance? Did it get lost in the river of years gone by? You know, love songs never die. They stay alive in us if we let them and they bring back such good memories. At our ages, we can enjoy the songs and the memories again and again."

"You know, we never picked a wedding song", said Mike. Laura said, "Oh yes we did. Don't you remember? We danced to the <u>Pine Tree Waltz.</u> That was our wedding song and everyone at our wedding loved it."

Mary stops reading again and says, "Hey, there is a note from William in the margin." It says, "My parents never liked to talk about sad events but I need to add a few events that shaped their lives."

"He listed several things, said Mary. I will read a few."

Child Births…My Mother used a midwife to deliver her babies. I say babies because she gave birth to four children over a 10-year period. I was the only child to survive the many sicknesses that plagued her early adulthood.

Prison Time…My dad spent two years in a Union prison designed for confederate soldiers. It took that long to process and verify his true identity as a northern spy. While there, he contracted smallpox and almost died. He was one of 40 that survived out of 300 Yankees.

Previously Engaged…My mother was engaged to a Yankee soldier before meeting my dad. She was to be married the month before she met my dad but her groom never showed up for the wedding. He was killed in action.

Two Lovers… Two young men were courting my mother after the Yankee soldier died. One was my dad, who was an ordinary man that did extra ordinary things in the Civil War. The other was Mark Twain, the famous author.

Mike & Mark

"I just wasn't sure that Mark Twain was the man for me. He was nice and he wanted to marry me but that wasn't enough. I didn't feel like I was home with him.

Mike made me feel like I had come home for the 1st time."

Mark Twain

Laura Travis 1874

Mary tells Jim, " There is no more of William's notes in the margin."

Bad Weather & Music

Laura remembers the weather and how very cold it gets in winter. She said to Mike " Remember that real cold day back in 73? I think it was January 29, 1873 - The morning low near Huntertown, Indiana was -34°.

This was the coldest day in recorded history (unofficially) in northeast Indiana. The low in Indianapolis was -13°.

We almost ran out of wood for the fire and it snowed like all get out, over 12 inches that day. This is why we should really seriously think more on moving away to a warmer climate."

Mike responded, "The best thing is the cuddling we did and the singing of all our love songs. We would have missed out if the weather were good. It was the bad weather that kept our song alive."

Laura agreed, "I guess so?"

Mike continued, "We always seemed to see the good in life, even when bad things happen. Yeah, we grumble a lot and cry a lot first, like everyone else but when it came right down to it, we chose to laugh and cuddle and kiss and love one another through it all. It must be our Godly perspective."

Laura agreed, "You are right. It's all based upon our belief in Romans 8:28 that God will work everything out for good to those that love Him and are called according to His purposes."

Mike replied, " That's us. We are the called ones to salvation and He watches over us to keep us in His grace. However, we are not the only ones."

The Bible says, "Whosoever" believes in Jesus is called of God. That makes us His children."

Laura replied saying, "That's why we sing all the time. We have hope in our hearts and we have peace because we found the love of God."

Mary stops reading to ask Jim a question. She says, "Hey Jim, what do you think about what they are saying in the journal?"

Jim replies, "Well, it seems that their love songs that never die are really their hearts singing to God. They seem to emanate from their love for each other in a continual flow to the throne of Heaven. It's pretty cool."

Mary comments, "What are the chances of us finding a journal from the 1800s that tells the story of a couple that argue, fight like cats and dogs, love like no tomorrow, and find happiness in the forgiveness of almighty God?

Plus, that blessed couple is your great, great, grandparents and my great, great, aunt. There must be a reason."

Jim replied again saying, "I think God wants us to carry on the love that Mike and Laura had. I think He wants us to be the Mike and Laura of our generation."

"Let's read some more", said Mary. She picks up where she left off.

"Laura replied saying, "That's why we sing all the time.

We have hope and we have peace because we found the love of God."

Mike Makes His Love Declaration

"Laura?, I need to tell you again how much you mean to me. It's in my heart and I have to express it before I burst." Mike looks a Laura and says,

"Oh how I love you,

From the bottom of my heart.

Come with me, my love,

And we'll chase away the dark.

Beyond the sorrow

And far above the stress,

Where we can be together

To enjoy life's very best.

Come my love

And lie beside me here,

So we can love forever

And dry up every tear."

More & Best

Then Mike kissed Laura and they drifted off into a gentle love feast. Laura began to say, "I love you too. I love you three. I love you four. I love you way beyond what I can count. But this I know for sure. I love you more."

"More?" Questioned Mike. Then he chased her around the house laughing all the way. They caught up with each other in the bedroom where Mike tells Laura, "You can love me more but I love you best."

The moonlight covered Mike and Laura and kept them through the night. Their passion lingered in an effortless ebb and flow as they held each other tight. They were lost in each other's arms until the sun began to rise over another a beautiful day.

This was their life and times when joy ruled their hearts and love was in the air. They were truly blessed of God.

No matter how trying life would be, Mike and Laura sang their love songs, believing that they would last forever.

Mary stopped reading. She wiped the tears from her eyes and said to Jim, "How beautiful is that? I want to carry on their love song. If God gave it to them over 100-years ago, He will give it to us, if we ask.

Don't you see Jim? Their love song is an expression of God's Love that shines through their lives together. This must have been what God wanted in the beginning when

He created man. That's why He created man as Male and Female, so they could sing His love song that never dies. That's why they were so happy."

The Hiding Place

"Listen to this", said Mary. "Mike and Laura are going to their hiding place. They don't say where it is, just that they are going there tonight. Listen!"

So Laura catches Mike's eye and says, "Hey Mike, let's go to our hiding place tonight. It's not far and we can spend the time together without all the hustle and bustle of city life."

Mike replies by laughing and saying to Laura, "City Life? We live in the country on a 150-acre farm. Our closest neighbor is the Peterson family and they are 28 miles away to the cast. How-e-v-e-r, I'd love to go to our hiding place with you."

You always make it fun and we have such a good time together. It's like going on vacation without traveling."

Jim says to Mary, "stop reading for a minute. There must be a secret place on the farm. If they do not have to travel, it must be here somewhere."

Mary replies, "I don't think so. We've been into the fields and are working in all the out buildings. I clean the farm-house and have been in every nook and cranny. It's not the chicken coop. Where else is there?"

Jim says, "It could be under the stars in the north pasture or along the south range where there are caves. It might be fun to do some exploring."

Mary answers, "Let's see if they mention any more about it." Mary continues to read but there was no mention of where their hiding place was.

Mike says, "I can remember the time we escaped the evil attacks on us from well meaning church folks that said we shouldn't have made wine."

Laura comments, "Yeah, we tried to tell them it was natural wine and was not tampered with to make the alcohol content a higher percentage. It was so much like grape juice but just a little fermentation to make it have a little zing. It was really healthy for you."

Mike continues, "Then there was that time when the tornadoes swept across central Indiana. We lost one of our out buildings and a sow. We made it through by the grace of God."

Laura again comments, "I remember a time when things were calm and the world was at peace and yet we escaped to our hiding place just the same because we were afraid that something might happen. Nothing did happen but we still were fearful."

Mike replies, "But it didn't and we still gave thanks to the Lord for protecting us and allowing us to be together and loving one another."

Laura comments, "Our, "Hiding Place" is the Lord. He surrounds us with songs of deliverence. We are safe when we are with Him. Remember the scripture, Mike?"

"Thou art my hiding place; thou shalt preserve me from trouble; thou shalt compass me about with songs of deliverance." Selah (Psalm 32:9)

A Suggestion

"Hey Mike", Said Laura, " Let's write our own love song, not just any song but one that will never die."

"Ok", said Mike, "I'll start."

> "In a twinkle of an eye,
>
> I fell in love with you.
>
> It was that twinkle in your eyes
>
> That drew me close to you.
>
>
> I was all alone, sad and blue
>
> Until you called out my name
>
> And said you loved me too."

"Hey, that's pretty good Mike", said Laura. "My turn, ready?"

> "Now the stars will shine-- most every night.

I see their twinkle, so starry bright.

They sing my love song --just for you

In a twinkle of an eye,

All my dreams came true."

"Very good Laura." Said Mike."Let's see if I can keep it going."

"In a twinkle of an eye

My life was made brand new,

Because you came into my life

And made a big "TO DO".

Oh how I love that you love me too.

It's that twinkle in your eyes

That keeps me close to you."

"Wow!" said Laura. How do I follow that? Here goes"

"Now our loves shines, oh so bright

All the day long and through the night.

Our love will last-- for all eternity

Even through the rain and the stormy seas."

Mike replies, "I'll finish it"

"I am so glad-- that I found you

In a twinkle of an eye

I fell in love with you.

Was that twinkle in your eyes

That made me say, "I Do"

Was that twinkle in your eyes

That made--- all my dreams come true."

"Hey, that's really good", said Laura. "Maybe some day it will get published and sung by lovers everywhere. What do we call our new song?"

Mike replies, "How about, The Twinkle Love Song?" Laura replies back to Mike,

"Yeah, that's ok by me."

And so The Twinkle Love Song became Mike and Laura's favorite. They wrote it down and made copies and put them with their most important papers so they would get handed down through the years. They made it a point to sing their new song to each other all the time.

Mary stopped reading as tears trickled down her cheeks. She said to Jim, "What a beautiful love song. We must get it published and known in our century. Mike and Laura would have wanted us to do that, don't you think?"

Jim replies, "Ok we'll do that as soon as we figure out the tune."

Mary said, "That will not be hard. My friend from church is a music teacher. She will know how to do it. Then we can sing it together as an expression of our love."

The next day, Mary took the song to her church friend and explained its origin and read the lyrics. She also tried to sing a little of it to a tune she had in her head.

However, when the friend listened to the words and a little of the tune, she immediately said, "I know that song. I found it in an old songbook published in the 18th century. A friend of mine republished it several years ago. He published it as a duet.

 My friend first sang it to his wife to drive away sadness and confusion when she was going through a tough situation. He said the tune just came out of nowhere as he prayed about what he could do to ease his wife's stress. He figured that it must have come from heaven because it worked."

So Mary and Jim obtained a copy of the song so they could sing it as a testimony of their feelings for each other. It became their love song, a song that will never die.

Mary and Jim put the journal down and retired for the night.

Chapter Seven

Tomorrow & Beyond

It's been two weeks since Jim and Mary have read from the 1800s journal. Mary wants to get back to learning more about Mike and Laura. She feels a strange sort of bond with Laura.

So Jim and Mary retire to the antique swing on the porch of the same farmhouse that Mike and Laura lived in more than 100 years before. They both felt a connection with their great, great, relatives when sitting on the swing.

Mary opens the journal to the place where she stopped two weeks ago. Jim settles in with a glass of iced tea and Mary begins to read.

"Laura?" Asked Mike, "What's tomorrow going to be like? At our ages, we seem to be living in the past among all our memories. We think of loved ones and friends that are now passed away and we dwell on happy or sad events that took place so long ago.

The "NOW" in our lives seems to be lost in the past. We are not dead. We are not even sick. We are alive and well on planet earth. Shouldn't we be living in the moment and thinking of the future?"

Laura agrees saying, "You bet-cha baby. It's time that we live again for the first time. So, what do you want to do?"

Mike responds by saying, "Let's stay right here on the porch, in this, our favorite swing, and continue to sip on a glass of iced tea as we contemplate the future."

Laura laughs and says, "Contemplate?

Mike laughs and says, "Yeah, you know, think profoundly and at length; meditate."

"OK" said Laura, "Let's do that."

Mike and Laura cuddled together on the swing and started kissing. It was just too good of a moment to let go by. They both laughed and Laura says, "We're supposed to live in the moment, right" That's what we're doing."

Mike says, "Tomorrow will take care of itself. Yesterday is gone and that leaves us with, "NOW" to live out each moment in time. It's our choice to laugh, cry, scream, be quiet, sit, stand or run. We decide our own "NOW" and that's how it should be.

Nations fight wars over this issue of deciding one's own destiny. Some folks want to take control. They are power grabbers that try to tell others what to think, what to do, and how to be. That's just not right."

Laura replies by saying, "However", to Mike's discourse. "We must remember what the scripture says in Galatians. (What so ever a man sows or plants he also reaps or harvests.) We must be doing good in our "NOW" so our future will also be good. They are connected.

Nobody gets away with doing bad things. God is not mocked. He will see to it that it comes back in a harvest against those that do evil?"

Mike jumped into Laura's thought process and said, "But kissing, being in love and making love are all good so they can't hurt us down the road, right?"

Laura says, "That's right but it could also be wrong. It all depends."

Mike replies, "Depends? On what?"

Laura answers by saying, "Well, if you are married, making love is seen as a natural expression of what God said to man in the beginning, "Be fruitful and multiply."

But if you are not married, God looks at making love as a sexual sin. He calls such people fornicators and plainly says that they will not enter into the kingdom of heaven. He puts those that fornicate in the same category as murders, witchcraft and those who are wicked."

So Mike was happy that he was in the will of God by being married to Laura. He believed that he was blessed above all men because he was Laura's heartthrob. However, he still had questions about tomorrow. In Mike's mind, tomorrow included death and whatever might be waiting beyond.

Laura sees a puzzled look on Mike's face and says, "What's wrong?"

Mike answers, "Well, I still am not sure about tomorrow. If we leave it to happenstance, we run the risk of complete chaos. Shouldn't we be planning and worrying about what may be ahead for us?"

Laura replies, "Jesus said to take no thought of tomorrow because our Heavenly Father knows what we need and will take care of us. That frees us from any real worry or anxiety about the future.

However, that doesn't mean we become lazy and unconnected with the future. We are just not to fear the unknown because God is in control of all of that stuff.

"We are encouraged to work out our own salvation as the Bible says. That will take lots of prayer, certainly obedience to what we know to be God's will and planning as a co-laborer with Christ to obtain our divine destiny.

What is beyond tomorrow is in the hands of God. He determines the outcome of life's events. You remember Romans 8:28, "God works everything together for good to those who love Him and to those He has called to be His children."

"There is one more scripture to think about. It's II Corinthians 5:8", "We are confident, *I say*, and willing rather to be absent from the body, and to be present with the Lord."

Here on earth, God watches over us. When we are absent from or leave our body in death, we immediately go to be with Christ. There is no space or time lag between death and life with God."

"You see Mike", said Laura. "There is nothing to be afraid of when thinking about tomorrow. It's all in God's capable hands."

Mary stops reading and asked Jim if all of what they are reading is true. Jim says, "Sure, it's all true. It comes from the Bible and the Bible is God's Holy Word. It is actually 66-books of truth.

Some folks deny the truth and say that the Bible is not a divine revelation that tells mankind about God and His love. However, I am not one of those folks. I believe and see Biblical truth as absolute. There is no gray area. If God said it, then it is and that settles it in my mind.

I was glad to hear that Mike and Laura were believers. We need to be more like them. They were truly blessed and I figure it was because they made Biblical truth their, "Life-Coach", to guide them through every day. They really practiced what they preached. Their lives and marriage were as an open book that anyone could read.

However, what they read and saw in Mike and Laura was the Love of God. The love of God must have emanated from them as a shining light. We sure see it as we read the journal. Imaging if we were there as an observer in real time."

Mary continues to read.

"I agree with you Laura about being in capable hands but I still have some unresolved issues."

Laura responds saying, "Issues, like what?" Mike opens up to Laura even more with a full list of "What About" things. He says…

"What about the Civil War and all the killing? It seemed to me to be a world out of control."

"What about the Small Pox epidemic 2-years ago that killed hundreds of children? What did they do to deserve a short life and so much suffering?"

"What about the train wreck that took the lives of 43 folks that were on their way to who knows where? They sure were not thinking of their future ending in a horrible death."

Laura simply smiled and said, "My dear husband, you error in your thinking to infer that these things were at God's direction or happened when He wasn't watching."

"Let's look at some Bible reasoning:

1. Man was created in the image of God. He had full control of his emotions and was given a free will to do as he pleased.

2. God is sovereign, meaning in full control. His full control gave man the right of choice and consequence.

3. Free will does not violate God's sovereignty. It is part of His full control so man can also experience his own sovereignty."

The Civil War was the result of man's exercise of his own free will. God did not want it. Nor did He sanction it. It happened because of man's greed and selfishness. God could not violate man's Sovereignty. If he had, man would be reduced to a animal, not a being in the image of God.

Sickness and disease, like Small Pox, does not come from God. It happens…and most of the time it is a result of man's unhealthy practices like drinking water stored in a barrel that has become full of germs. God is a God of love and peace and mercy. He does not take pleasure in our suffering.

The train wreck was also a result of man's free will. God didn't make the train. He didn't stretch out defective rails for the train to run on. There is always a reason for things that happen. Sometimes we do not see it right away but it is still there waiting to be discovered.

Some folks blame God for what happens instead of realizing that He is actively working behind the scenes to bring some good out of the bad that happens.

Tomorrow is fast approaching but we need not fear its arrival. God is with us to help us meet every challenge and to overcome every obstacle. He loves us and wants only to bless us so we can in turn be a blessing to others."

Mike lets out a sigh of relief and says, "Thank You" to Laura.

Chapter Eight

The Wedding Party

JIM AND MARY ARE STILL sitting on the swing reading his great, great grandparent's journal. Mary continues to read.

Mike and Laura are finally getting back to the wedding party and renewing their vows after 50 years of married life.

Mike asked another question, "Hey Laura? Do you think we will be married in heaven? Some religions say a man can have lots of wives in heaven. It makes his status greater."

Laura replies, "So how many wives do you want, Mike? You can't handle the one you have now. You are always telling me I am a handful. How many hands will you have to fill in heaven?"

Mike laughs and says, "That sort of stuff is not for me. I was just saying."

So Laura goes to the Bible, their source of truth to answer his question. She says, "Let's look at what Jesus said to the Sadducees when He walked the earth. (Matthew 22:23-32) It's time for a little Bible Study"

"The same day came to him the Sadducees, which say that there is no resurrection, and asked him,

Saying, Master, Moses said, If a man die, having no children, his brother shall marry his wife, and raise up seed unto his brother.

Now there were with us seven brethren: and the first, when he had married a wife, deceased, and, having no issue, left his wife unto his brother: Likewise the second also, and the third, unto the seventh.

And last of all the woman died also. Therefore in the resurrection whose wife shall she be of the seven? for they all had her.

Jesus answered and said unto them, Ye do err, not knowing the scriptures, nor the power of God. For in the resurrection they neither marry, nor are given in marriage, but are as the angels of God in heaven.

But as touching the resurrection of the dead, have ye not read that which was spoken unto you by God, saying, I am the God of Abraham, and the God of Isaac, and the God of Jacob?

God is not the God of the dead, but of the living."

Mike, after hearing the words of Jesus says, "so there is no marriage in heaven, right." Laura responds by saying, "No, there is marriage in heaven. It's just not to each other.

Haven't you heard that the church is the, "Bride" of Christ and there is going to be a marriage feast in heaven where Jesus receives His bride? We are the bride of Christ. That's how we inherit the kingdom of God, It will come through marriage and so shall we all be with Him."

"We are now joint heirs but then we will be joined in spirit as one, forever to rule with Christ. Now that's a great future to look forward to."

Mike says, "But what about us? Laura explains, "US" will be with all other true believers. Us will be better than what this life could ever offer. Imagine being, "One Spirit" with Christ and ruling over everything God has or will ever have. That's a pretty big deal."

Laura changes the subject saying, "Our wedding party should not be restricted to a weekend. We could have it on a weekday as well. It is all the fashion now.

Our wedding was in the morning, remember? at around ten a.m. The location doesn't have to be a church. We held our wedding in my uncle's home. It was popular to hold weddings in the home then because it allowed a more exclusive and intimate affair."

"I remember", replied Mike, "Like other home weddings, we did the traditional thing, to hang symbols of good luck like wishbones, horseshoes and bells over the place where we exchanged our vows. That was a fun thing to do."

Laura said, "Back then brides did not wear white for their weddings because the color was too expensive and impractical. Modern bleaching techniques did not exist. However, now I can wear white if I want. I don't have to wear colors like before.

I wore my Sunday best as you did. Having a separate dress to wear for just one occasion was extremely impractical, especially in a world without the mass-production of textiles as we have today.

I am still wearing that plain gold band you gave me. It was very uncommon for both the bride and the groom to exchange rings. We had only one wedding ring and it was for me. Maybe this time you can wear one too. It seems to be fashionable for a mam to wear a wedding ring now a days. We can have our initials engraved in the rings with the date we were married."

"Remember the reception, Laura?" said Mike, "It was just after we got hitched. Because it was so early, we had to provide breakfast for everyone. There wasn't enough chairs for folks to sit. Only our bridal party could sit and eat. This time we should hold our reception in a hall so everyone can sit down."

"Times are different now than when we were married", said Laura. "Back then it was custom and deemed proper etiquette for the guests to address the bride first, unless they didn't know her, in which case it was the groom's job to introduce them to her after receiving their congratulations. We didn't know any of that sort of tradition. We just went ahead and got married."

We did not have any entertainment at our reception or wedding: it wasn't needed then as it was commonly understood that it was an honor just to have been invited to share the day.

Our guest did, however, get cake. I made a dark, rich fruitcake with white frosting. We did not eat the cake at the reception. It was cut and boxed at the end of the day and passed out to the guests as they left."

Mike says, "Yeah, I remember that and I also remember the shoes. When we left for our honeymoon we were pelted with rice and shoes.

Yeah, shoes thrown at us by the guests. They said it was a symbol of wishes for fertility and happiness in our marriage. I thought it was pretty strange."

Laura replies, "We'll just have to tell everyone not to toss shoes at us this time. Besides, we are not leaving for a honeymoon. We are staying with our guests and dancing and having fun."

Mary stops reading again and talks to Jim saying, "there were some strange customs back then. I guess 100-years of progress can make a difference."

Jim replies, "Now let's see. It has to be more than

100-years. They were married in 1870. The journal is a record of their 50th year together. That would put the date around 1920. We are living in the year 2020. That's 150 years from their wedding day. If they were married in their 20s like most folks were, they should have been around 70-ish as they plan for their wedding renewal party."

Mary replies back to Jim, "So what does that have to do with anything?" Jim replies, "Well, it has a lot to do with the story of their lives.

Consider this: they lived in the, "Roaring Twenties." It was a time of gangs, crime, gross immorality and corruption.

Mike and Laura were senior citizens in a fast changing world where law and order was stretched to its limits and God was being pushed out of human society. I wonder if they realized how much and how fast their world was changing?

We can look back and see the things that affected their lives. I can think of a few off the top of my head:

1. The Civil War must have had a profound effect on them.

2. The world was again at war when they were planning their party (WWI)

3. A president was assassinated during their life-time. (Abraham Lincoln)

4. The 5th amendment was ratified that gave black males the right to vote.

5. The telephone and the electric lightbulb were invented.

6. The fountain pen, the farris wheel and Coca Cola were made.

7. Crayons, cotton candy, the air plane, the automobile and the radio all came into existance.

Unfortunatly, they had to confront the theory of evolution that emerged in 1859. World values were changing rapidly and Mike and Laura lived through a time of cahos.

The beauty of it all was that even though everything around them was in a state of rapid change and not all for the good, they remained true to their convictions and continued to walk in faith before God."

Mary concludes, "And we thought we had it tough. Their world was much like ours but harder in many ways."

Jim and Mary retired for the night vowing to continue reading the next day.

The next day came and it was business as usual for Jim and Mary and Mike and Laura. Both couples settled on the swing that hung on the porch. They sipped their glasses of iced tea in the moonlight and continued to ponder life's most challenging questions.

For Jim and Mary, it was the discovery of their family ties to their great, great, grandparents. For Mike and Laura, it was what to do with the rest of their lives.

Mary opens the 100-year old journal and Mike and Laura come alive again as she reads the remaining pages.

Mike says to Laura, "I wonder if our names and lives will be remembered a 100-years from now?"

Laura responds, "We are nobodies in a sea of nobodies. Why would we even think we would stand out to be remembered? We didn't invent anything. We didn't discover a cure or strike it rich."

Mike laughs and says, "Fame and notoriety does not come from what you do. It comes from who you are. The fact that you are here at this time and in this place with me is a miracle. It was destined by God. He has taken note of us and inscribed our names on the palms of His hands and written our names in the "Lamb's Book of Life.

The point is, Laura, that if no one remembers us, God does. He will never leave us or forsake us in this world and throughout eternity."

Mike continues, "That's really good for us to know. It is comforting to realize that we are indeed in His hands and are His beloved children. We are certainly not descendants from monkeys.

Darwin must have been crazy or was it just a way for him to become famous? He tried to remove God from man's thinking entirely.

When you say man evolved through a transmigration process of species, you deny God His rightful place as the creator of all things. To do so is Blasphmy."

Laura asked, "I am not sure what that means" Mike explains, "Blasphemy is the act of insulting or showing contempt or lack of reverence to God.

This theory will diminish the value of human life and open a door for mass extinction of people that society deems worthless. God help us in the years to come."

Mary pauses her reading. She is crying. Jim asked why and she responds, "Because of the babies. Mike was right about mass extinction. Over 60 million unborn children have been eliminated, denied a chance to live because they were deemed to be worthless.

Plus Six million Jews were exterminated in WWII because they too were deemed worthless. What has happened to our world? Have we all gone crazy?"

Jim replies, "Yes honey, we have gone crazy. That's what happens when man denies God His rightful place. They somehow fall into debauchery and evil arises to rule the day."

So Jim and Mary retire for the night and Mike and Laura

return to the pages of the journal until they are opened again.

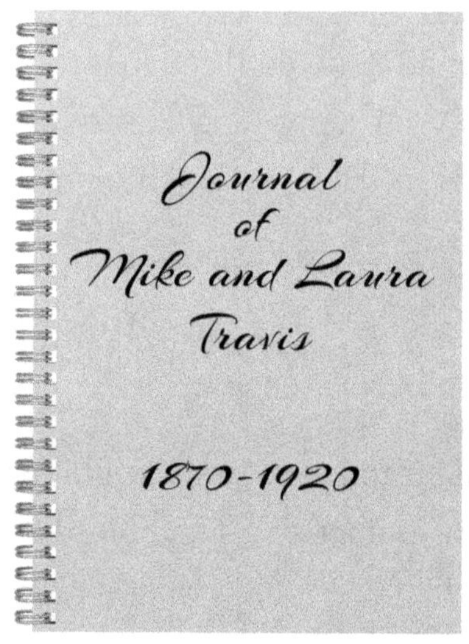

Chapter Nine

Times And Seasons

MARY WAS WOKEN FROM A deep sleep with the voice of Mike in her head. He seemed to be talking way off in a distance. She kept hearing Mike say, "Hey Laura, What time is it?" She immediately woke Jim and asked him if he heard voices. Jim said, " no."

Mary explained what she heard and said that it was Mike's voice talking to Laura. She also said that the voice was coming from the swing on the porch.

So Jim and Mary got up, took the journal and went to the porch. Jim said, "This is silly. We are following a voice in your head."

Mary said, "Do it anyway, for me. I need to know. I heard Mike ask Laura, what time is it?"

Jim said, "Who cares. Let's go back to bed. It's 3:00 AM." But Mary said, "Be quiet and listen as I read."

Mike asked Laura, "Honey, what time is it?" Laura said, "It's time for us to be alive and to breath and to laugh and to cry and to pray and to praise God. This is our time and it's for two, you and me. We are the "Times Two Generation."

Mike said, "I guess there is a time for everything. Isn't that what the Bible says?"

Laura agreed and read from her Bible Ecclesiastes 3:1-2-4-6-7-8-13-14-16-17

1"To every thing there is a season and a time to every purpose under heaven.

2 A time to be born and a time to die; a time to plant and a time to pluck up that which is planted;

4 A time to weep, and a time to laugh; a time to mourn, and a time to dance;

6 A time to get, and a time to lose; a time to keep, and a time to cast away;

7 A time to rend, and a time to sew; a time to keep silence, and a time to speak;

8 A time to love, and a time to hate; a time of war, and a time of peace.

13 And also that every man should eat and drink,

and enjoy the good of all his labour, it is the gift of God.

14 I know that, Whatsoever God doeth, it shall be forever: nothing can be put to it, nor anything taken from it: and God doeth it, that men should fear before him.

16 And moreover I saw under the sun the place of judgment, that wickedness was there; and the place of righteousness, that iniquity was there.

17 I said in mine heart, God shall judge the righteous and the wicked: for there is a time there for every purpose and for every work."

Mike comments on the reading, "We are surely in His hands. He rules the times and the seasons putting them at our feet. We are surely the "Times Two" generation when God blessed us with each other and His matchless love.

How often do we say, Is it time yet? Or what time is it? Or It's high time. We are creatures of time. We live by the day or month or year, counting every moment and judging it to be good or bad. How many times have we said, We had a good time or The time will come."

Laura joins in by saying, "Now is the acceptable time. It comes from II Corinthians 6:2 which say… "(For he saith, I have heard thee in a time accepted, and in the day of salvation have I succored thee: behold, *now is* the accepted time; behold, now is the day of salvation.)

These are powerful words. They speak of life, death, salvation, good and evil and final judgment."

Mike seeks an answer, "Where are we in all of this?" Laura answers, "We are in Christ Jesus, hidden from the world and all its chaos. We are living in the blessings of God's grace and are protected from the wrath of God that is to come upon the world."

Mary paused her reading and she and Jim talk about what Mike and Laura are discussing.

Mary asked a question, "What does Laura mean by "Protected?"

Jim replies, "It all rests on what God has said to his children in the pages of the Bible. He never said that he would protect the wicked. However, Paul, the apostle said to the church, "For God has not appointed us for wrath, but to obtain salvation through our Lord Jesus Christ." I Thessalonians 5:9

We can rest assured that if God's destiny for us is to obtain salvation, we will not suffer His wrath. Salvation is true deliverance. We are delivered from God's wrath because we put out faith and trust in Jesus.

This was His plan from the beginning and is the good news of the Gospel. Thus, we are "Protected" because we believe."

Mary replies to all Jim said, "But I don't feel saved or protected. We live in troubled times when murder, rape and other evil acts happen all around us. I do not feel safe, do you?"

Jim answers, "As I see it, safe is a state of mind, a perspective that is built on the Word of God.

What if I told you that God has placed His personal angel at your side to protect you because you reverence Him? Listen to the scriptures,

"The angel of the LORD encamps round about them that fear him, and delivers them." Psalm 34:7

When God's personal angel encamps, he sets up his camp of warring angels all around you. The purpose for this action is to deliver you from evil and the wrath of God that is falling on the wicked.

If we can receive what is being said, we can rest in the Lord, knowing He is there for us. How do you feel now?"

Mary said, "Better," "I guess this is why Mike and Laura are so happy. They are resting in the Lord and have no worries about tomorrow."

Jim responds saying, "That's right. They are living life in God's blessings because they have decided that what the Bible says is true and they can count on it to shape their reality."

Mary says, "We need to do the same. Mike and Laura

are not only our great, great, relatives. They are also our examples to learn how to rest and believe. Praise God for their testimony. Let's continue reading."

Mike said, "These are our times and this is our season to laugh and love and rejoice in the Lord. The good news is that our season does not have to change. We know that God is on our side. He will help us get through whatever befalls us. He even says, *"Be it unto you according to your faith."*

Even if, God forbid, one or both of us die, we will be with the Lord in His Glory."

"Mike", said Laura, "Where did the times and seasons come from and why are we subject to them? It seems that we should be living in one season and one time, not many. What do you think about that?"

Mike answers by saying, "Let's look into the scriptures and see if we can find a Biblical answer instead of me tossing out my unlearned opinion. "Here we go, I found several references:

Genesis 1:14 - *And God said, Let there be lights in the firmament of the heaven to divide the day from the night; and let them be for signs, and for seasons, and for days, and years:*

Genesis 8:22 - *While the earth remaineth, seedtime and harvest, and cold and heat, and summer and winter, and day and night shall not cease.*

1 Thessalonians 5:1 - *But of the times and the seasons, brethren, ye have no need that I write unto you.*

Acts 1:7 *And he said unto them, It is not for you to know the times or the seasons, which the Father hath put in his own power.*

Psalms 104:19 *He appointed the moon for seasons: the sun knoweth his going down."*

"Well, based upon the Word of God, said Mike, Times & Seasons were established by God in the creation to separate light from darkness, day from light and season from season. He must have wanted different seasons so man would not get bored. He also established them for as long as the earth exist.

The apostle Paul said that we have no need to question. We should already know that it was God's will and therefore we should accept it and enjoy it.

I figure it this way, God divided time in order to keep track of it? It was His will that we work. He knew we would need to rest. The spring, summer, autumn, and winter seasons offer a dependable cycle where we can live out our lives in some sort of orderly fashion. Also, the times and seasons help us to relate better to the past and the future.

Day and night, months, and years were part of God's original creation before sin entered the human experience.

He even gave mankind the seventh day of the week to rest from all his labor.

All of the past generations were keenly aware of their dependence on the times and seasons and the regular patterns of sun, moon, and stars.

They trusted that the sun would rise every day and bless them with crops. Without the seasons, life on earth would cease to be.

Unfortunately many past civilizations worshipped the sun and moon and stars instead of God, who created them. But we know that day and night is founded on the unchanging nature and promise of God (Numbers 23:19).

The times and seasons remind us of God's faithulness. We know the sun will rise and winter will always follow the fall.

We also know that each new day brings a fresh new opportunity to start over again because God's mercies are new each morning. We get a do over every day to grow in His grace and fix whatever went wrong the day before.

The Scripture says, *"He makes his sun to rise on the evil and on the good, and sends rain on the just and the unjust."*

Praise the Lord that each new day is an opportunity to put the past behind us because of his great mercy.

God didn't have to bless us with times and seasons but he

did. That's why we love to sit in the moonlight and watch the sun rise. It is the handi-work of our Heavenly Father."

Mary pauses again to talk to Jim saying," I didn't know why God made the times and seasons. It was for us, right?" Jim responds, "That's right, Mary"

Jim continues, "I'll bet you didn't know that our seasons are the result of the earth's tilt on its axis.

I think it is also a Spiritual thing to get mankind accustom to change because change is evident in life. It is the only thing that is constant. We need to learn how to deal with it.

Does that satisfy your curiosity, Mary?" "Yes", she said and then continues, "However, we are bound by time and God is not. We suffer under the change of the seasons being too hot or too cold or whatever. I guess we will have to live with all the change, as did Mike and Laura in their day."

Jim replies, "Yep, we will, but you know what I see? I see different times depicted by different events, some to man's betterment and some to his dishonor. Let's pray that our times will not be remembered in history for man's evil actions.

It would be nice for future generations to read about us with a sense of peace and honor because we followed after righteousness."

Mary replies back and says, "In Mike and Laura's day, their times were full of hardship, war and evil but they still had a sense of peace and lived in their own God built reality."

It was sorta like Noah's Ark. God's love and grace provided an Ark, or Hiding Place where they could find safety until the storm diminished and peace was restored."

Mary and Jim closed the journal and return to bed with a new outlook on the love and mercy of God.

Chapter Ten

As Time Goes By

IT'S BEEN THREE WEEKS SINCE Mary and Jim opened the journal. They have been busy planning their own 1st wedding anniversary party.

Jim looks over at Mary and says, "Time sure has passed by us this month. It's been three weeks since we looked at my great, great, grandfather's journal. Now that we are married, I can really relate to Mike and his fascination with Laura."

"Fascination?" said Mary

Jim replied, "Yeah, man is always fascinated with the opposite sex and especially when the opposite is his wife. I am fascinated with you.

It's like this, when God made woman, man was asleep. He missed out on all the particulars that cause her to work. God forgot to give man an instruction manual.

Most men, including me, haven't even got a clue. That's

why we are so fascinated, ever trying to figure out what makes women tick.

You are so very different, like Laura of 100+ years ago." Mary responds, "How am I like Laura?" Jim says, "Like in a lot of ways." Mary pressed Jim for more details saying, "Explain!"

So Jim starts to formulate a list of ways Mary is like Laura, based upon what they have read so far. "OK", said Jim, "Here we go:

1. You, like Laura, are independent. You can take care of yourself.

2. You, like she, are smart, no airheads here. You think things out.

3. You, like her, are about the same size and hair color. Both of you are and were pretty.

4. You, like Laura, chose a great guy to marry, Mike and me respectively.

Need I go on? I just love you and that's a fact. It's my story and I am sticking to it."

Mary says to Jim, "We have some time. Let's read some more from the journal." Jim agrees and they settle on the porch in the swing as most all the other times. Mary begins to read.

"Hey Laura", said Mike, " Time is sure passing by fast. Tomorrow is our wedding anniversary party. We'll get to see all our families, friends, neighbors and even some guests that are friends of guest that we do not know. It's going to be a full house. Have we forgotten anything?"

Laura responds, "No, it's all under control. All we have to do is show up. We decided not to rent a hall, remember. The Barn is larger and more suited to us and our guest. It will be the biggest barn dance in history."

Mike says, "Yeah and the biggest "Pot Luck" supper ever. It's taking 10 long tables to place all the food. I told everybody that there would be no booze and no smoking in and around the barn."

Laura replies saying, "There is a national ban on booze. We do not want to be arrested for breaking the law. Besides, faith in God and booze do not mix."

As the time goes by, Mike and Laura finalized everything for the party. Then they cuddled up together on the porch in the swing as always and enjoyed each other. The moonlight showered them with beams of harvest gold and the evening slipped into the darkness of night. All was well and peace ruled over their little farm.

The next day, a trail of female workers kept coming and going to and from the Travis barn. It looks somewhat like a beehive with worker bees buzzing around everywhere.

They brought cookers, place settings, more decorations

and all the fixins for a party. Laura had her hands full for most of the day. Mike still had farm duties and worked hard to finish them before party time. Finally, the hour had come.

"Are you ready Laura?" said Mike. "Let's do this. You and I will stand at the barn entrance and greet folks as they arrive. The band will play upon our signal, when there are 15 or 20 people in the barn."

Laura said, "I have my gals all in place manning the food tables, punch bowl and even the cookers. Oh yea, there are a few boys on trash patrol. They are the only paid help."

Mike responds, "Look Laura, the Johnson's are the first to arrive."

As time goes by, the barn filled with people and the music played. The Pine Tree Waltz was a big hit as always. It was one of the most popular songs during the 1870s when Mike and Laura were married. You might say that it was an oldie from the past.

Suddenly and without warning it began to thunder and lightning. The barn remained dry but outside was a torrent of rain, wind and fire.

Laura called to Mike, "Mike, don't go out there." Mike replied, "I have to see how bad things are because folks are parked in areas that turn to mud when it rains."

So Mike runs out into the storm that was overhead, only

to hear a boom in the sky and to see a tree hit by lightning and fall on the barn.

Mike cried out, "Oh my God!" as his guests fled the barn. The tree crushed the roof leaving a gapping hole and a fire broke out flooding the barn with smoke.

Mike ran over to Laura who had established a make shift 1st aid station near the farmhouse. He says, "Are you OK" She answers, "Yes but at least a dozen guests were injured. Thank God no one died."

"I witnessed a miracle tonight", said Laura. "How so?" said Mike?

Laura explains, "Well I was sitting right where the tree fell. It actually came crashing down on top of me. I couldn't get out of its way. But when I thought it was all over, I cried out to the Lord for help and He heard me.

Mike? I saw an angel, a real angel, standing right beside me. He was holding up the tree so it wouldn't crush me and it was on fire. He also breathed on me, pushing the smoke away from my mouth.

The angel looked at me and smiled as if to say, "Get out of this place." So I ran and made it out safely. God protected me."

Mike said, "That's incredible, a real angel? Wow! Well we lost the barn but saved everything else. We even have smoked ham thanks to the fire." "That's funny", said Laura. "Smoked ham, huh?"

So Mike and Laura's 50th wedding party ended in disaster but they chose to see the good instead of the bad. Mike said, "The barn can be rebuilt but the people cannot."

Laura said, "No one was seriously hurt. It could have been really bad but God saved the day with only one angel."

Their faith and trust in God brought a new blessing the following week. The same folks that danced at their wedding party and got stuck in the mud and had to flee for their lives, showed up with lumber and tools and volunteers to begin reconstruction of the barn.

The volunteers numbered more than thirty and they simply said, "This is our wedding gift to you."

Mary stopped reading in amazement. "Did you hear that, Jim? A real angel. How interesting is that? There is an angel in your family's past. Do you think it was her Guardian Angel?"

Jim was slow to answer as he was thinking. Then he spoke up, "There is no convincing evidence in scripture that every person on earth has their own specific guardian angel.

There are angels who protect, guard and minister to God's people (Psalm 91:11-12), but the wicked have no angels of God to protect and guide them.

They have only demonic spirits that seek to torment them, kill their dreams, steal their peace and destroy their destiny.

I am convinced that angels exist. I believe in them because the Bible plainly teaches that they exist. From Genesis to Revelation we read all about angels.

At least 250 Bible passages speak of angels. The last book of the Bible alone has 80 references. Hebrews 1:14 describes them as "ministering spirits." However, God allows them to come in the appearance of man while they are communicating with people on earth. They minister to the needs of the saints, not the wicked."

Jim says to Mary, "What happens next to Mike and Laura?" Mary opens the journal and reads on.

Mike and Laura settle again in the swing that is on their porch to cuddle and give thanks to God for His help during the storm. Laura says, "Look at that Mike? God has given us a bigger and better barn than we had before plus I saw an angel."

Mike replies, "That's right Laura and life will go on and we will be alright. We are in His hands and no one can pluck us out.

By the way, one day soon, when we are walking the streets of heaven, we will see lots of angels. In that day, we will be able to talk to them and laugh with them and worship with them. They are our friends, for sure."

Laura tells Mike, "We will wait and watch, as time goes by, and maybe next year we will have another wedding party."

Mike agrees and makes a suggestion, "How about one every year? They can all bring gifts. We can call it the 5th annual wedding party of Mike and Laura Travis." Laura jumps in and says, "What? Are you crazy? Don't be silly and don't repeat that suggestion to anyone."

Mike and Laura shift gears and begin looking to the future. Mike says, "We should consider the future, Laura. The big question is, "What now? Where do we go from here?"

Laura has an idea. She says, "How about going somewhere, like the Deep South where it is warn year around and we can fish off the beaches? We do not have to move, just visit for a while and see if we like it."

Mike says, "What about the farm?" Laura responds, "William can handle it. It will be his one-day when we are gone. He can get some first hand experience."

So Mike and Laura leave their son in charge and drive their pickup truck south. They had no idea where to stop but just kept driving. Laura said, "I will know when we get there. God will show me."

They stopped in North Carolina for the night and left in the early morning for parts still unknown.

As time goes by, they finally reach a little town on the east coast called Boca Raton in Florida.

Mary paused again saying, "They went to Boca when it was a little place. It was first incorporated on August 2, 1924 as "Bocaratone," and then incorporated as "Boca

Raton" in 1925. It is now one of the wealthiest communities in South Florida. The 2018 population estimated by the U.S. Census Bureau was 99,244.''

Mary continued reading, "Now Mike and Laura spent several weeks playing in the surf and building sand castles on the beach. Their favorite pastime was to hunt for shells at the water's edge.

Mike and Laura loved the area so much that they purchased beachfront property. It wasn't very expensive because it was deserted beach, totally undeveloped.

Jim says to Mary, "Wait a minute. That property today must be worth a fortune." Mary responds, "There are all hotels along the beach now. They must have sold it somewhere along the way. Can you imagine owning Boca Raton Beach?"

Mary continues to read the last part of the journal.

Mike and Laura lived out their lives in central Indiana. They stayed on the farm where they could still enjoy their friends and family, especially their grandkids. They let their son manage their affairs so as not to have the burden of the farm. It was paid for and prosperous.

Mary closed the journal and looked at Jim saying, "I guess that's all. We do not know how long they lived and what transpired beyond 1920."

"One thing is for sure", said Jim, "Mike and Laura lived a great life and enjoyed the blessings of God's grace all their lives. They stood as a testimony to their world and stand today as a testimony to you and to me that God is real, Jesus is alive in our hearts and the Holy Spirit is leading us towards our divine destiny."

Conclusion

EVERYONE WANTS TO BE HAPPY. However, many people are not. They seem to be sad, depressed, burdened down with worry and anxiety and just not pleased with how life is treating them.

I think the problem lies with where one has his or her eyes. Listen again to what Helen Keller said.

"When one door of happiness closes, another opens, but often we look so long at the closed door that we do not see the one that has been opened for us." —Helen Keller

I use her quote because it typifies the core problem with those that are not happy. They spend too much time looking at closed doors instead of searching for the open door that God has waiting for them.

We have been looking back and forth through time, listening to Mike's great, great, grandparents celebrating their 50th wedding anniversary in 1920 and observing one young married couple who are their descendants that live in the same farmhouse more than 100 years later.

The young married couple discovers the secrets of true

happiness. They also find God's grace and faith to live in a modern world of political correctness, immorality and selfishness.

God called Mike and Laura, as he does all believers, including Jim and Mary, according to His divine will or purpose.

As Christians, we love God because He first loved us and saved us from our own sin. The scripture says, if we love God and are called by Him, He will work everything together for good, even the hard times and trial we face.

The end result is good, not evil. That means the damage is repaired and we become more complete in Him.

Although Jim and Mary and Mike and Laura were more than 100 years apart, they had a special bond, a sort of fellowship of mind soul and spirit.

What lies ahead for Mary and Jim will be built upon the Word of God. It is their heritage passed down through the years first to Mike and Laura and finally to them.

Their Christian values stand as a testimony for new believers and weary souls needing refreshing in the Spirit.

The End

About The Author

John Marinelli

Rev. Marinelli is an ordained minister, He has formed and been pastor of one church in Wisconsin and was the pastor of another in Alabama. He has also been a youth minister and evangelism director over the years.

Rev. Marinelli has authored several books including: "Original Story Poems", a children's story poem book, "The Art of Writing Christian Poetry," and "Pulpit Poems." He is also the author of "Mysteries & Miracles", a Christian fiction story. He further authored over 80 eBooks on various Christian subjects. They are all free downloads from his website;

www.christianliferesourcecenter.org

John is an accomplished Christian poet. He also dabbles in songwriting and writing one act Christian plays.

He is the Vice President of Have A Heart For Companion Animals, Inc., a "No Kill" animal welfare organization.

Rev. Marinelli is now retired from the sales and marketing arena after spending over 40 years in business-to-business and non-profit marketing.

Rev. Marinelli enjoys writing Christian fiction stories, playing chess, singing karaoke and a retired lifestyle in sunny Florida.

For More Info or eMail Contact
johnmarinelli@embarqmail.com

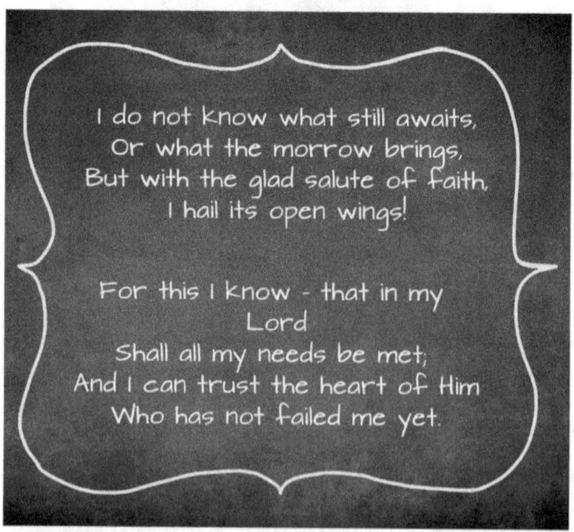

Gallery
of
Christian Poems
Anointed Christian Poems
By Rev. John Marinelli

All Creation Waits

A blue-gray sky
Winks at the dawn,
As the morning light
Sings its glorious song.

Life is flourishing everywhere,
Unaware of what's in store.
The sounds of spring beckons,
In a silent and peaceful roar.

Time marches onward,
Towards the brink of day,
As all of creation waits
For God's children to pray.

By John Marinelli

Don't Worry

Don't worry about tomorrow.
You did that yesterday.
Go on with your life
And remember always to pray.

Ask and it shall be given to you,
But this great truth you already know.
Rejoice and be happy, why? Because
Your harvest comes from what you sow.

I will say it again and even more,
Until it becomes very very clear.
Tomorrow will take care of itself,
But worry is another word for fear.

Now here's what I want you to do.

Trust in the Lord and be of good cheer.
Drop the worry from your vocabulary
And cast out that demon of fear.

By John Marinelli

Arm's Length

I hold the world at arm's length,
That its choices do not interfere.
While it does its own thing,
I watch and wait over here.

My steps must not go that way,
For it's not where I need to be.
The Lord has shown me the path,
That will lead me to my destiny.

The call to follow is strong
And pulls at me now and then.
But I know that way
Is full of sorrow and sin.

I must move on in life
Beyond their beckoning call.
It's the right thing to do,
So I do not stumble or fall.

I will not be swayed or misled
By family, friends or business deal.
Their secret thoughts are not mine,

To consider, to admire or feel.

So I keep the world at "Arm's Length"
As I journey through this life.
My faith in Jesus keeps me strong,
As I walk in His glorious light.

By John Marinelli

Clutter

Clutter keeps the mind confused,
As images dance through the night.
Lost among those unimportant thoughts,
Are the dreams that once shined bright.

An endless parade of fear and doubt,
Crowds the mind to destroy our day.
Ever soaring on the wings of the soul,
Until it has formed an evil array.

But clutter is by one's choice,
Of those who dance to its beat.
Better to face imaginations' due
Than to fall into utter defeat.

By John Marinelli

The Lord's Little Two By Four

God has a little 2' X 4'
That rest on heaven's windowsill.
He uses it now and then,
When we stray from His will.

Sometimes we need a good "Bap";
With the Lord's little 2' X 4'
To knock out the confusion,
And help us to desire Him more.

The Lord's little 2' X 4'
Is what we sometimes need,
To get our thinking straight,
And keep our focus indeed.

The Lord's little 2' X 4'
Is fashioned from life's every trial,
So we do not stray from His will,
Or fall into an ungodly lifestyle.

By John Marinelli

I Find Myself In God

I find myself in God.

He is my, "Everything"

I know that He is Lord,

My Life, my Hope, and King.

I find myself in God,

Not the ways of Sin.

Nor do I look to others,

To know who I really am.

I find myself in God,

To whom I bow on bended knee.

He alone is my joy and strength

And where I want to be.

By John Marinelli

"I Am" There

"I AM" There,
At the end of your broken dreams,
Before the sun rises over your day,
Prior to those tear-filled streams.

"I AM" There,
Down that road of despair,
When all appears to be lost,
And no one seems to care.

"I AM" There,
Over all of life's twists and turns,
When tomorrow is all but gone,
And when you are full of concerns.

"I AM" There,
Sayeth the Lord of Host,
To bring you hope and peace,
And the power of My Holy Ghost.

"I AM" There,
To be sure you make it through,

In the midst of every trial,
To bless your life and deliver you.

"I AM" There

By John Marinelli

The Pastor &
The Master

If the pastor doesn't follow the Master,
Then I cannot follow the pastor.
But if the pastor walks with the Master,
Then I can walk with the pastor.

When pastors stray from the Master,
The sheep will stray from the pastor.
But when the pastor loves the Master,
God blesses the sheep and the pastor.

Jesus is the pastor's Master,
And why the sheep follow the Master.
For He is Lord over the pastor.
That's why they call Him Master.

The pastor and the Master--
The Master and the pastor--
The sheep follow the pastor
When the pastor follows the Master.
By John Marinelli

The Lighthouse

A lighthouse is a blessing,
To the ships that toss in the sea.
For it shows them the way,
Until they can clearly see.

The rage of an angry storm,
Cannot hide its brilliant light.
Nor can its awesome fury,
Rule as an endless night.

Jesus is the lighthouse,
For those who have gone astray.
The light of His love,
Offers a new and living way.

Jesus is the lighthouse,
When fear and sickness rage.
The light of His love,
Gives hope in difficult days.

So trust in the Lord,
And look for His light.
He alone is "The Lighthouse",
That guides you through the night.

By John Marinelli

The "Way Maker"

Only Jesus can make a way,
Through the difficulties of life.
He alone is Lord and King,
Over life's sorrows and strife.

He is the "Way Maker,"
When there is no visible way.
He will make the way known,
As though it were the light of day.

He will make a way,
For those of humble heart.
He will clear away the rubble,
Restoring what Satan broke apart.

Jesus is the "Way Maker,"
A friend to all who are lost.
He has made the way,
Paying sin's incredible cost.

The way to the Maker,
Is through His only Son.

He alone is the "Way Maker,"
Until life's battles are won.

By John Marinelli

Wise Men Still Seek Him

Wise men still seek Him
Who appeared so long ago.
They come now by grace
Through faithful hearts aglow.

Wise men still seek Him
For He is their "Bread of Life."
A sustaining inner strength
Through times of sorrow or strife.

Wise men still seek Him
The Christ of Calvary.
God's only begotten Son
Crucified as Sin's penalty.

Wise men still seek Him
Jesus, God in human array.
King of kings & Lord of lords
Born to earth on Christmas Day.

By John Marinelli

A Highway Called, "Holiness"

He places my feet on
A highway called "Holiness,"
That led my soul
To the throne of God.

Amidst the cheers of angels,
I walk, wearing His holy gown.
Onward towards heaven's throne,
While evil cast its awful frown.

My eyes were opened
That I might see.
Both the good and the evil,
That sought after me.

I walk the highway-Holiness
That crosses all of time
Towards the throne of God
Leaving this world behind.

By John Marinelli

The Angels Cry "Holy,"

The Angels cry "Holy,"
While sorrow fills the land.
For God's Judgment Day,
Is to come upon every man.

The Angels cry "Holy,"
While mankind goes astray,
Rejecting the love of God,
To follow his own precarious way.

The Angels cry "Holy,"
Knowing the terror of the Lord,
When all who dwell in sin,
Will suddenly be destroyed.

The Angels cry "Holy,"
Waiting for all things new,
Born of the Holy Spirit,
When God's Judgment is through.

The Angels cry "Holy,"
"Holy is the Lamb,"

Waiting for the children of God,
To join "The Great I AM"

By John Marinelli

Call Upon The Lord

When your burdens overwhelm you,
Like a mighty raging sea.
Call upon the Lord, Jesus,
And He will set you free.

When your heartaches are many,
And life is difficult to understand.
Call upon the Lord, Jesus.
He will come and hold your hand.

When your friends reject you,
Because you follow after Him,
Call upon the Lord, Jesus,
And keep yourself from sin.
When you fall into depression,
As though it were a giant pit.
Call upon the Lord, Jesus,
Who will restore your joyful wit.

When you're saddened by the day
Feeling lost and all alone.
Call upon the Lord, Jesus,
Who will make His way known.

When you're weary and heavy-laden
Tired from life's many tests.
Call upon the Lord, Jesus
Who is sure to give you rest.

By John Marinelli

It Came To Pass

It Came

Things often come to pass,
But seldom do they ever last.
They come into our busy day,
For awhile, then pass away.

We hear their voices, loud and clear,
When they arrive and while they are here.
They speak both joy and misery,
Some to you and some to me.

We say, "It came to pass,"
Or say, "It happened so fast."
Down life's beaten path,
Comes both love and wrath.

So say goodbye to sad and blue.
To all that is now troubling you.
For things will come, only to pass,
But God's love will always last.

By John Marinelli

Rest My Child

Take your peace and be restored
Then put your faith in Jesus, the Lord
He has provided, your mouth to feed.
From the beginning, He knew your need.

Do not worry, fret or even fear,
for, my child, He is always near.
To bless your soul with love and grace,
To be with you, face to face.

Come, my child, near to His throne.
Do not allow your faith to roam.
For those who will not believe,
Can never find rest in times of need.

His word will see you through.
His grace He freely gives to you.
That you should rest, your soul to keep,
Forever delivered from unbelief.

By John Marinelli